RACE CARS

By Jenny Devenny, LCSW

Edited by Charnaie Gordon

Frances Lincoln
Children's Books

AUTHOR'S NOTE

Race Cars originated through my Masters in Social Work and was an attempt to answer my own questions about how to talk to kids about race, as I navigated working as a white therapist with predominantly Black children and families. Since then, I've been delighted to see readers of all ages and races using the book as a tool to jump-start discussions. I am thrilled to collaborate with Charnaie Gordon to bring out this thoughtfully updated edition.

My hope in writing *Race Cars* was to support BIPOC [Black, Indigenous, and People of Color] children in resisting social messages of racial inferiority and to support white children in developing a positive self-concept that enables them to like themselves without needing to feel superior to anyone. My goals are for children to recognize unfairness, develop the emotional empathy to know that bias hurts, and to feel empowered to disrupt racism in their own lives.

Race Cars is purposefully simplistic. It is meant to be read often, and as part of a library of diverse books that foster self-love and celebrate differences. The more you read this book the more you will get out of it, so don't be discouraged if your first conversations don't go as planned. Children want to know more about unfairness, and how to make an unfair situation fair, and will give you plenty of opportunities to try again. Thank you for taking this important first step.

—Jenny Devenny, LCSW

EDITOR'S NOTE

In recent months, discussions about racism, bias, and white privilege have been at the forefront of our everyday lives. Many people avoid these discussions because they fear that conversations about these topics lead to feelings of guilt, anger, discomfort, sadness, and at times disrespect. The current state of our world, however, no longer allows for these tough conversations to be ignored. That is why I decided to take this project on and edit this story in collaboration with author Jenny Devenny. I am so happy with how this story has evolved and I hope YOU as the reader will enjoy it too.

While uncomfortable for some, we are in a position to lead or at least participate in tough conversations with children. It is my hope that readers will use this book to engage in constructive dialogue about privilege, prejudice, racism, and the ways that all of us can work together to shift the conversation from hate and violence toward understanding and respect, to ultimately bring about positive change and unity to our communities.

In addition, I hope white children recognize that having privilege does not require them to feel guilty for their privilege. Use this book as a conversation starter to discuss how privilege looks in our society and which groups have privilege, and which do not.

As with any book, *Race Cars* is meant to help springboard conversations. It is still up to each person committed to racial justice and equality to do their part. There is still so much more work to be done, but I believe the work is worth our time, effort, and energy, because our children's lives are at stake. Thank you for reading and supporting this important book.

—Charnaie Gordon

TIPS FOR READING RACE CARS WITH KIDS

Stop and think critically: When reading the story, stop at various points to give children a chance to discuss what's happening. Refer back to what you already know about the characters and encourage children to make predictions based on this information. For example: *"We know that Chase is a black car and that the organizers of the race want a white car to win. What do you think they might do to make sure he doesn't win? Is that fair?"*

Reach for feelings and activate children's moral imaginations: Have children consider what the characters in the book might be feeling as they read the story. *"Can you imagine what Chase must be feeling in this moment? Has anyone else ever felt like that?"* Encourage them to think about what they would do in that situation. *"If you noticed something unfair happening, what could you do? Where could you find help?"*

Invite full participation: When discussing difficult topics such as race, some children may tend to shut down, whereas others may dominate the conversation. Pay attention to non-verbal cues such as body language or facial expressions to get a better sense of how children are reacting to the story, in order to create space for reactions and voices that might go otherwise unnoticed.

Relate it to the wider world: *Race Cars* is a fictional book, but the book is a reflection of the wider world. Formula 1, the world's most famous race-car championship, is one of the most expensive sports to participate in, which explains why most Formula 1 drivers are white and come from rich families. In 2007, Lewis Hamilton became the first (and still only) Black driver in Formula 1 history. Overcoming racist treatment throughout his career, he has gone on to become the most successful driver in the sport. Lewis is unique, not only because he is Black but because he also comes from a working class background. Lewis is fighting to become more involved with Formula 1's governing body (similar to the committee in *Race Cars*) in order to change the rules to be more fair. Lewis is also a supporter of Black Lives Matter and anti-racism within Formula 1.

In the NASCAR Cup Series, the top racing circuit in America, Darrell "Bubba" Wallace is the only Black driver. In 2013, he became the first African-American in 50 years to win in one of NASCAR's top three national touring series. Bubba has played a critical part in NASCAR's push for inclusion and equality. In May 2020, after the killing of George Floyd by police officers in Minneapolis, Wallace spoke out about the unfair treatment of Black people by the police, and called on NASCAR to ban the Confederate flag at NASCAR races. The Confederate flag, a symbol of slavery and white supremacy, was officially banned on June 10, 2020.

This is Chase.
Chase is a black race car.

This is Ace.
Ace is a white race car.

They live in a world with lots of other race cars.
Big ones, small ones, short ones, tall ones,
old ones, new ones, brown ones, blue ones.

Chase and Ace have been best friends forever.
For as long as they can remember they have been training
together for the world-famous, annual race-car race.
Last year, they were finally old enough to enter the race.

For as long as anyone could remember, every year when the big race came around, a white car would win the race. A white car would win fourth place, third place, second place, and first place. Until last year…

Last year, Chase won first place and Ace won fourth place. Sometimes competition can come between friends, but not for these two. Ace was so happy for Chase, and Chase was so happy for Ace. They loved to race and did not care about place.

There were, however, some cars that **did** care about place.

These cars were on the race committee.

No one had ever seen them, but everyone knew who they were. They were a group of white cars that made all the rules for the annual race-car race.

When the committee heard about Chase winning, they were not happy. A black car had **never** won first place. They did not want things to change.

"We have always given white cars the fastest tires and the most powerful engines!" they roared. "How could a black car have won?"

For the next race, the committee decided to change a few of the rules to make it easier for the white cars to win and harder for all the other cars.

They all agreed except for one... Grace. Something about it didn't feel right to her. She was used to things not feeling fair—after all, Grace was the youngest committee member, and the only girl! But she didn't say anything because everyone else felt so strongly.

Next year rolled around and Chase and Ace
were ready to race again. They had spent all
summer training and knew the route by heart.

Chase started off faster than ever. He zipped around the track as the crowds cheered him on.

Once around the track.

Straight through the cornfield.

Over blue mountain.

Through the magical forest.

Chase was getting ready to cross the bridge when he noticed a sign that had not been there before.

"Bridge is for white cars only. All other cars must go around the river." Chase paused for a second. "Hmm…that's strange," he thought, but he did not want to waste any more time.

Chase sped around the river as fast as he could and jumped over the finish line.

Even without taking the bridge, Chase managed to come in second place. Ace came in first place. Ace was so happy for Chase, and Chase was so happy for Ace. They loved to race and did not care about place.

Bridge is for white cars only

But back at home, something was bothering Chase. It just did not seem fair that the bridge was for white cars only. Was he not as good as the white cars? Was something wrong with him? He shrugged it off and decided to train even harder for next year.

Back at Ace's house, Ace was snuggled up in bed smiling. He did not expect to be faster than Chase—in their practices Chase was always fastest. "I must be getting much faster," thought Ace. He drifted off to sleep dreaming of next year's race-car race.

And back at the committee, the white cars were still not happy that Chase had won second place. They decided to change more rules to make it even easier for the white cars to win—and even harder for all other cars to win. Grace didn't think it was fair, but she didn't want to lose her place at the table, so she stayed silent.

The next year rolled around and Chase and Ace were ready to race.

Chase started off faster than ever.

He zipped around the track as the crowds cheered him on.

He made it to blue mountain
in the blink of an eye.

Then he whizzed through the
cornfields in record time.

But at the top of the mountain a race officer stopped him.

"Pull over please, I need to see some identification."

Chase paused for a second. "Hmm…that's strange," he thought, "none of the white cars seem to be getting stopped," but he did not want to waste any more time. He showed the officer his identification and continued the race through the magical forest.

Chase sped around the river as fast as he could and jumped over the finish line.

But because the race officer stopped him, Chase did not place, and Ace came in first instead.

Chase was happy for Ace, but they were both upset about Chase's race. They loved to race and did not care about place, but the committee had just announced a new rule. Cars that did not place this year could no longer race next year...

Next year Chase **would not** be allowed to race.

Back at home, Chase was devastated. He did not care about place, but he loved to race—what would he do now? Chase could not help feeling like he was not as good as the other cars—he felt like something was **definitely** wrong with him. Why else would he not be allowed to race? That night, Chase cried himself into a long, deep sleep.

Back at Ace's house, Ace was snuggled up in bed, but something did not feel quite right. He did not understand why Chase did not place. "He is the fastest car I know!" thought Ace.

Next year would not be the same without his best friend. Chase was the reason that Ace liked to race in the first place! Ace sighed, shrugged his shoulders and drifted off into a long, deep sleep.

Back at the building where the race committee held their meetings, Grace tried to speak out against Chase being pulled over in the race. She knew it wasn't fair and some of the members agreed, but others didn't.

"We need to change the rules of this race to make it fair and equal for all!" said Grace, softly.

"Yes, we agree!" whispered two more cars. But most remained silent and ignored her. They were afraid of change and did not want to lose their space at the table.

START

He zipped around the track as the crowds cheered him on.

Next year rolled around and Chase was at the race to cheer his best friend on.

Ace started off faster than ever.

Then he whizzed through
the cornfields in record time.

He made it up blue mountain
in the blink of an eye.

Ace was heading for the magical forest when something made him pause. A forked road with two separate paths—one for white cars and another for all other cars. "Why have I never noticed this before?" thought Ace.

Ace wanted to know what was down the other path. He wanted to understand what the race was like for Chase.

Ace took a right and went down the longer path instead of the shorter one. He sped off into the magical forest, faster and faster until he realized that he was lost.

White cars

All other cars

Back at the track, the race committee was starting to get worried.

All the cars had finished the race except for their star race car, Ace. Where could he be? The race officers looked everywhere but could not find Ace.

The committee decided to hold a meeting to figure out the best way to find Ace. "We need the fastest race car," said one. "The fastest race car should surely be able to find Ace."

"But Ace **is** our fastest car," said another.

"**NO!**" shouted a voice from the back of the room. The committee turned to see where it had come from. It was Grace and she could not stay silent anymore. This time they would listen.

"The fastest race car is Chase, even though we did not ever let Chase have a fair race," said Grace. "Take down those unfair signs! If we let Chase race at his fastest pace, he will definitely be able to find Ace!"

START

He zipped around the track as the crowds cheered him on.

Although Chase was still upset that the committee did not allow him to race this year, he quickly agreed to help save his best friend.

"Here I come, Ace!" said Chase.

He made it up blue mountain in the blink of an eye.

Then he whizzed through the cornfields in record time.

When he got to the magical forest he saw Ace
speeding towards him.

"I'm sorry it took me so long to realize how much
harder it was for you to win this race, Chase," said Ace.

The best friends **embraced**!

Then, together, Ace and Chase finished the race.

DISCUSSION NOTES

pp10-11

Can you think of any places in your own life where mostly white people are in charge of making the rules or have power? (School? Our government?)

Why do you think the race committee was so upset that Chase won the race?

What do you think some other reactions to him winning might have been? (For example, how might other black cars have felt seeing him win?)

Note to adults: This could be a good time to explain what racism means to your kids. *"Racism means unfair treatment of people based on a lie that says one race is better than another. This story is not real, but in real life, white people in many countries created a lie hundreds of years ago. This is the lie of **white supremacy**, or the belief that white people are superior to or better than BIPOC because they are white and it is a lie that has affected and influenced a lot of the laws and rules that have been written in many countries. Because of the lie of white supremacy, white people often get privileges that they do not earn and that BIPOC do not have. Over the years there have been movements to change the rules and make things fair for everyone. During the civil rights movement of the 1960s, Black leaders like Martin Luther King Jr. fought to change the rules and won. Unfortunately, even after the rules changed, some white people created different rules to stay in power in secret ways. Also, because people were so used to those rules and so used to believing the lie behind those rules they sometimes still act like those rules are true and white people still get unfair benefits."*

pp16-17

When Chase is getting ready to cross the bridge he notices a sign that says "Bridge is for white cars only."

Who do you think put that sign there? Why?

Can you think of any real life situations where the rules are different for one group versus another group? Is this fair or unfair?

What do you think it felt like for Chase to see that sign?

What do you think Ace thought when he saw the sign? What would you do if you were Ace and you started to see that the rules were different for you than for your friend?

Note to adults: This might be a good time to start defining white privilege for your kids. *"In this book, the white cars get special privileges that the black cars do not. Privilege is a special benefit not enjoyed by all. Even though Ace did not ask for these privileges, he is still benefiting from them simply by being a white car. The same is true for people as well. Because of the lie of white supremacy, white people often get privileges that they do not earn and that BIPOC do not have. We call this **white privilege**. White privilege is not something that white people necessarily do or enjoy on purpose, but it is something that they all benefit from."*

Can you think of some advantages that people get because they are white? When you cut your finger do the "flesh-colored" bandages match your skin tone?

pp18-19

What is the difference between Chase's and Ace's reactions to the race? How does Chase feel? How does Ace feel?

Ace does not seem to notice all of the extra barriers Chase has to go through to finish the race. Why do you think he might not realize what Chase is going through?

Why does Ace think he is winning the race, and not Chase?

Why is Ace really winning the race?

Grace is the youngest committee member and the only girl. How do you think this may have helped her to recognize unfairness in the race? Why do you think this might have also made it harder for her to speak up about the unfairness?

pp22-23

What do you think is happening here?

Why did Chase get stopped and not Ace?

What do you think Ace would have done if he saw Chase get stopped? What would you do?

Note to adults: This could be a good time to connect the story to events that kids may be noticing in real life. *"This story is not real, but in real life our skin color affects the way we are seen by others and how we are treated. Another part of the lie of white supremacy was the lie that white people made up that said Black people are dangerous. Even though we know this is a lie, there are some people that still believe it. Other people don't think they believe it, but still act like they do. This often leads to white people calling the police on Black people when they are not doing anything wrong and the police treating Black people unfairly."*

pp24-25

How does Chase feel about not being able to race?

How does Ace feel about his friend being out of the race?

How do you think this will affect their friendship?

What would you do if you were Ace?

What would you do if you were Chase?

pp32-33

The committee changes the rules to allow Chase to race in order to save Ace—do you think they would have changed the rules if Ace was not in trouble? What do you think will happen next year?

From what we know about this committee, do you think they will make the rules fair?

What do you think the race would be like for a brown car? Or an LGBTQ car? In the real world we have many different identities, some of which are less visible than others but can also impact the way we are treated.

What should they do? What would you do?

In real life, racism is still happening and white people are still getting privileges that they did not earn simply because they are white. The rules that made things harder for Black people keep changing and also keep staying the same. How can something keep changing and staying the same? What do you think that means? What can we do about it?

Dedicated to Dr. Willie Tolliver,
who taught me how to talk about race. —J.D.

Source references: *"Anti-Bias Education for Young
Children and Ourselves" by Louise Derman-Sparks and
Julie Olsen Edwards*

Brimming with creative inspiration, how-to projects, and useful
information to enrich your everyday life, Quarto Knows is a favorite
destination for those pursuing their interests and passions. Visit our
site and dig deeper with our books into your area of interest:
Quarto Creates, Quarto Cooks, Quarto Homes, Quarto Lives,
Quarto Drives, Quarto Explores, Quarto Gifts, or Quarto Kids.

First Published in 2021 by Frances Lincoln Children's Books,
an imprint of The Quarto Group.
100 Cummings Center, Suite 265D, Beverly, MA 01915, USA.
T +1 978-282-9590 F +1 078-283-2742 **www.QuartoKnows.com**

A CIP record for this book is available from the Library of Congress.

ISBN 978-0-7112-6290-4

The illustrations were created digitally
Set in Helvetica

Publisher Katie Cotton
In-house Editor Katy Flint
Designer Sasha Moxon
Production Controller Dawn Cameron

Manufactured in China TT022021

9 8 7 6 5 4 3 2 1